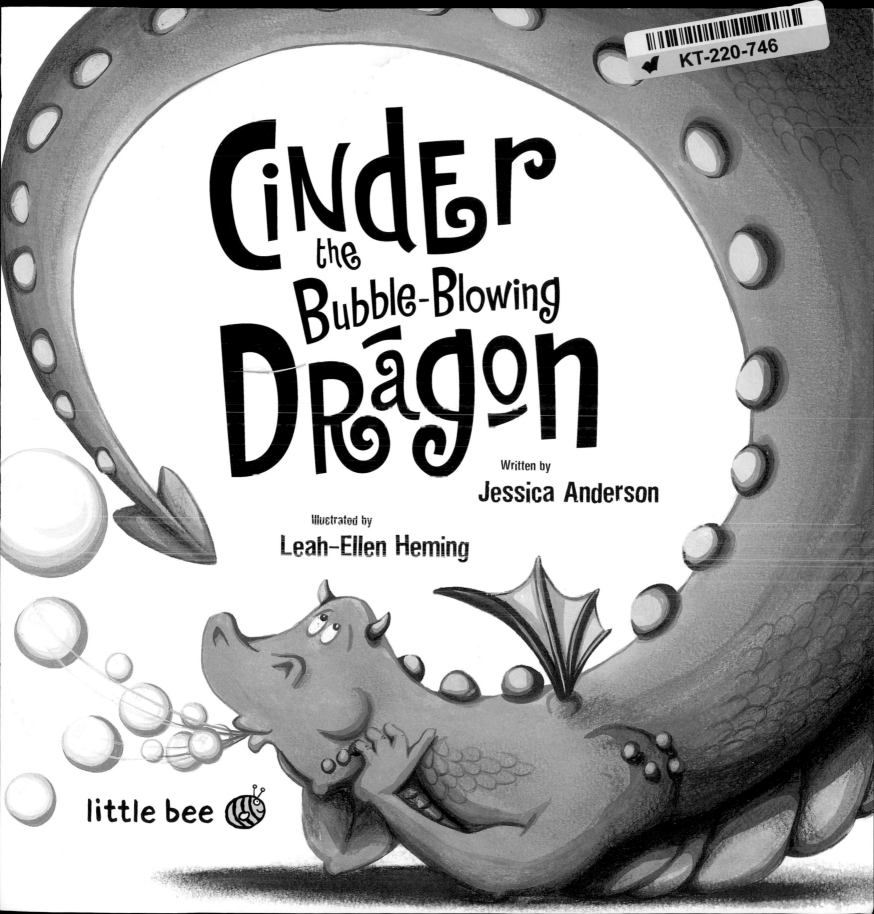

CINDER
the
Bubble-Blowing
DRAGON

Written by
Jessica Anderson

Illustrated by
Leah-Ellen Heming

little bee

"This simply won't do," said the King. "You'll have to go."

He shook his head so hard that his crown toppled over one eye. But Cinder, the King's Dragon, didn't dare to smile.

"What sort of dragon are you, anyway?" the King continued. "All the other kings have proper fire-breathing dragons while I, **KING OF TARRAGONIA,** have a dragon who can only blow...

...**bubb**les!

It's just too embarrassing."

The King was right,
thought Cinder.

He was a sad
disappointment.

Coming from a famous dragon
family, great things had been
expected of him.

But when he became the junior dragon at the palace, he found he could only blow bubbles...

...and however hard he **puffed** and **snorted**, not one flicker of flame appeared.

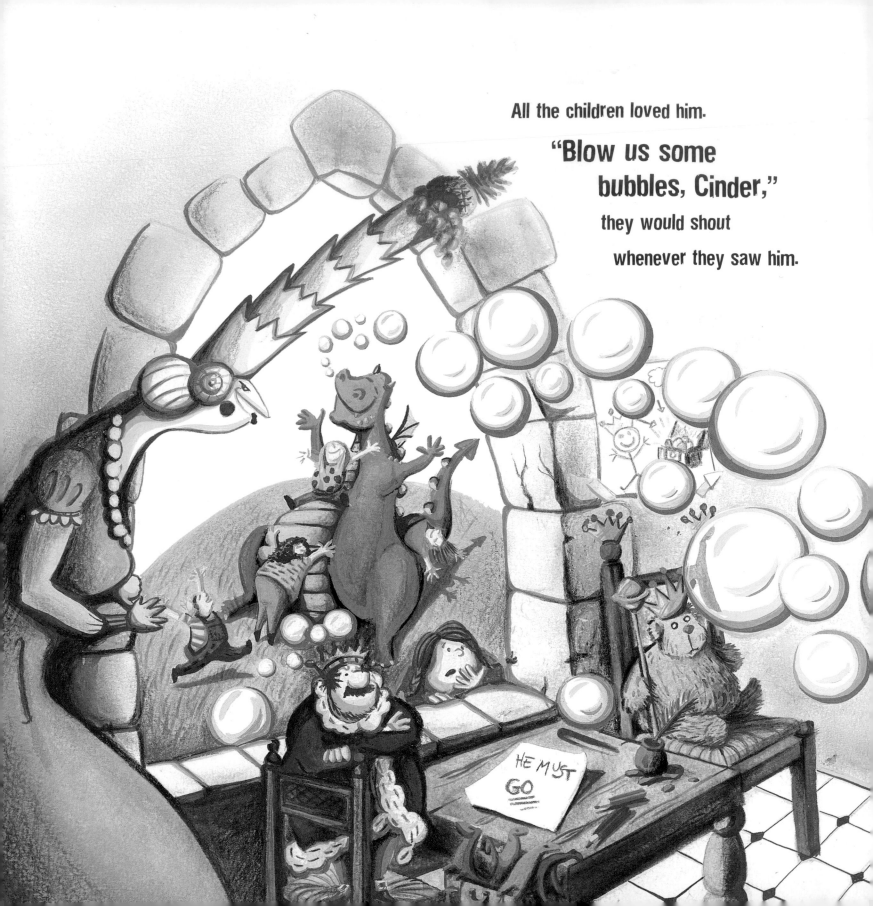

All the children loved him.

"**Blow us some bubbles, Cinder,**" they would shout whenever they saw him.

They thought bubbles were much better
than fire, but the King was not amused.

Now he'd decided that Cinder must go.

He'd even put an advertisement
in the **"Tarragonia**
Times".

It read:

WANTED
A fire-breathing
DRAGON
for palace duties.
Applicants must be able to
produce large quantities of
SMOKE AND FIRE

One dragon had applied.

"When he comes this afternoon you may be present in the Throne Room to see how a real dragon behaves," said the King.

At two o'clock there was an enormous **roaring** at the palace gates.

"Blaze, the World's Most Fearsome Dragon, wishes to see the King,"
bellowed an enormous voice and the air filled
with smoke and flames.

"**OK, OK,** show-off, keep your
fireworks for the King," snapped the palace sentry crossly.
He was fond of Cinder and thought it was a shame he had to go.

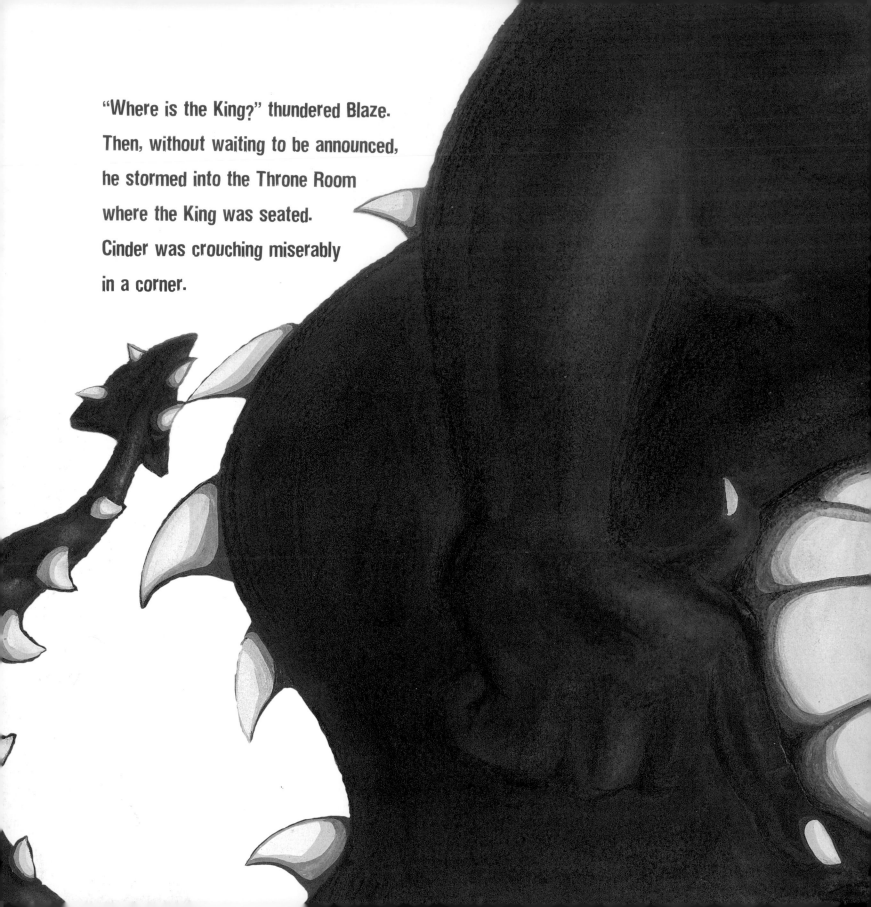

"Where is the King?" thundered Blaze. Then, without waiting to be announced, he stormed into the Throne Room where the King was seated. Cinder was crouching miserably in a corner.

The King looked rather alarmed as the creature's hot breath reached him and frizzled his beard.

Then the carpet started smouldering and flames crept up the curtains

When his crown began to melt the King had had enough.

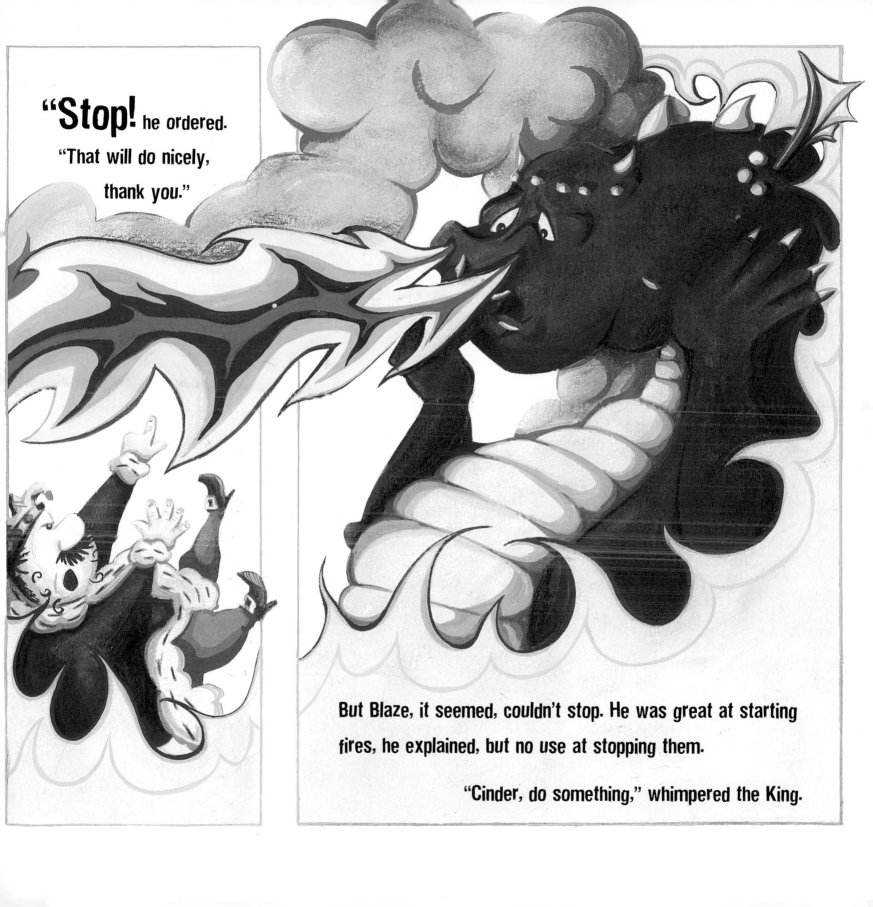

"**Stop!** he ordered.
"That will do nicely,
thank you."

But Blaze, it seemed, couldn't stop. He was great at starting fires, he explained, but no use at stopping them.

"Cinder, do something," whimpered the King.

Cinder did the only thing he could think of. He blew with all his might and, as the bubbles began to fill the room the flames died down, the carpet no longer smouldered and the Royal Crown stopped melting.

"Now I've done it," thought Cinder.
"I've quite put out Blaze's fire."

Blaze himself was pretty put out too,
but the King was delighted.

"Thank goodness you were here,"
he said, as he ordered a dish of
ice cream to cool himself down.

"Some people don't know what they want – even when they get it," muttered Blaze huffily as he departed in a cloud of very black smoke.

"I don't hold with all this smoke pollution," said the King as he gobbled his ice cream.

It appeared the next morning
and read:

For Seonaid with love

J.A.

For Mum, Dad, Alex, Anthony,
my dearest friends
and the Kool House

L-E. H.

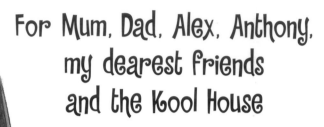

First published in 2006
by Meadowside Children's Books
185 Fleet Street
London EC4A 2HS

This edition published in 2007
by Little Bee,
an imprint of
Meadowside Children's Books

A CIP catalogue record for this book
is available from the British Library

10 9 8 7 6 5 4 3 2
Printed in China